LUA THE LLAMA
AND THE MOUNTAIN OF JOY

Written by Alison Birks

Illustrated by Linda Weston

Type, layout & design by Debra Atwater

Dedication

For the Q'ero and for the children of Pachamama

Lua the llama lived in the high Andes mountains of Peru.
Each day Lua did what all of the other llamas did:
she grazed on grass, climbed the high rocky terraces,
chased other llamas and then she slept under the stars.

Day after day, week after week, month after month,
year after year, Lua lived as all of the other llamas have always
lived, until one night, when Lua had a strange dream.
She dreamed of a beautiful, shining Rainbow Llama, who said:
"Lua, you are so much more than just a llama!"

The next morning, Lua was very confused.
Wasn't she simply a llama like the rest of them?
Yet somehow she felt that the Rainbow Llama was
telling her the truth. She was something more –
but who was she?

She would ask Mama Llama,
for surely she would know who she was!

Lua found Mama Llama grazing in the sunlit grass.
"Who am I?" she asked Mama Llama, in earnest.
"Why, you are my little Lua" Mama Llama said sweetly.

"But I am more than that! Who am I REALLY?"
she questioned.

Mama Llama sighed. "You are a llama. You are meant
to graze on grass, to climb the high rocky terraces,
to chase other llamas and to sleep under the stars.
I'm sorry Lua, but I don't know what you mean.
Ask Papa Llama. He will have the answer."

Lua went to see Papa Llama, who was very busy
searching for fresh grass to eat.

"Papa Llama, who am I?" asked Lua.
"What do you mean?" asked Papa Llama, as he grazed.
"You are my little Lua and you are
Mama Llama's little Lua" Papa said firmly.

"But I am more than that! Who am I REALLY?"
she demanded.

"You are a llama. You are meant to graze on grass, to climb the high rocky terraces, to chase other llamas and to sleep under the stars. Sadly, I do not know what you mean. Ask the old healer don Paqo. He will know."

Filled with hope, Lua journeyed for many days and nights high up into the mountains searching for the one the llamas called don Paqo.

Finally, she found him alone, making prayers. Don Paqo
was as old as the stones and very wrinkled, but his
sparkling eyes were youthful. He seemed kind and wise.

"Who am I?" asked Lua, excitedly. Don Paqo gazed at Lua, then closed his dark brown eyes and was silent.

After what seemed like eternity, he opened them
and looked squarely at the little llama.
"That is a very big question Lua and it deserves
a very big answer," said don Paqo.
"But I can't tell you who you are. I can only show you."

Lua looked puzzled.

Don Paqo laughed and said, "Come Lua, let's take a walk.
The earth is soft from the rain, the grass is lush and
the sun is shining brilliantly. It is a perfect day for a walk."

They walked for a long time, as don Paqo
taught Lua the ways of his ancestors.

"Now listen closely little Lua to the teachings of my people."

"When you think good thoughts
for the world, then you will have Yachay—Wisdom."

"Yachay?" wondered Lua.

"When you show love and kindness to the world,
then you will feel Munay—Love."

"Munay?" mused Lua.

"When you choose a life of helping others
then you will know Yanchay—Service."

"Yanchay?" repeated Lua.

"And when you give before taking,
you will know Ayni—Balance."

"Ayni?" repeated Lua, still looking puzzled.

The wise don Paqo laughed.
"Come Lua, Let me show you."

Lua and don Paqo stared at the trail ahead
and both started to climb. They climbed higher
and higher up into the mountains until finally
they reached Putukusi — the Mountain of Joy.

Lua watched as don Paqo made a k'intu,
a prayer bundle of three perfect leaves.
He blew prayers of gratitude and love into
the k'intu before offering it to the mountain.

Don Paqo prayed and prayed. He prayed for himself.
He prayed for his family, for his community
and for the llamas. He prayed for the mountains.
He prayed for the well-being of the whole world
and he prayed for Lua, too.

Lua watched don Paqo and tried to do the same.
She pushed leaves into uneven piles of three with her nose
and blew her llama breath onto them.

With her little hooves she kicked up the k'intus
into the wind then prayed aloud –

"Munay Earth!" proclaimed Lua,
"Munay Pachamama!" whispered don Paqo.

"Munay Sun!" snorted Lua,
"Munay Inti Tayta!" taught don Paqo.

"Munay Moon!" exclaimed Lua,
"Munay Mama Quilla!" said don Paqo.

"Munay Stars!" shouted Lua,
"Munay Hatun Ch'aska!" affirmed don Paqo.

"Munay Mountains?" wondered Lua,
"Yes Lua, Munay Apus," laughed don Paqo.
Lua smiled.

In the joy of that moment, Lua suddenly knew that
the whole world was alive and filled with light.
She and don Paqo prayed together with the k'intus.
The sun, the moon, the stars and the mountains seemed
like dear old friends, who had been waiting a long time
for Lua's visit. Even the stones were smiling.
Everything was alive!

The sun was setting by the time don Paqo
finished making his prayers and the two began
the long hike back down the mountain.

As the two friends began their descent,
Lua looked back to see Putukusi, the Mountain of Joy,
beaming forth a ray of pure pink light.
The light bathed Lua and don Paqo in its loving radiance.

Lua's heart was filled with great peace as she basked
in the light from the heart of the mountain.
Just like don Paqo, she felt love for the whole world.
Her mind was clear and she knew her place in the world.

She was a llama. She was Mama Llama and Papa Llama's
little Lua, but she was also so much more!

"Don Paqo, I have found my SELF!" Lua snorted excitedly,
"And I am so much more than just a llama!
I am part of a whole universe filled with light and
love and my place in the world matters!"

Don Paqo smiled. "Yes Lua, now you know
the truth of who you really are!
From this day forward
you will be known as Rainbow Llama."

"You will bring the teachings of
Yachay, Munay, Yanchay and Ayni
back to Mama Llama, Papa Llama and the others,
so that they will learn the truth, too!
Munay Lua!"

Lua was overcome with gratitude and love for don Paqo,
for the llamas, for the world. Her eyes welled up
with tears of happiness as she gazed upon Putukusi,
the Mountain of Joy, one last time.

"Munay Putukusi"

She turned again to thank the wise one who had brought her to the Mountain of Joy and who had taught her the ways of his ancestors.

"Munay don Paqo!" called Lua.
Don Paqo just smiled, and in a flash
of mysterious light, he was gone.

Andean Glossary
(abbreviated from www.incaglossary.org)

Apu: (n) The spirit of the sacred mountain; the most powerful of all nature spirits.

Ayni: (n) Reciprocity, balance, harmony. Right relationship; sacred interchange. *"Today for you, tomorrow for me."*

Ch'aska: (n) Star *(usually Venus)*

Hatun: (n) Great

Inti Tayta: (n) Father sun.

K'intu: (n) A little fan of three cocoa leaves representing the three worlds brought together in prayer for an offering; a bouquet. The k'intu is a symbol of the integration of body, mind and heart working in ayni within the center.

Mama Quilla: (n) The moon as an expression of the divine feminine.

Munay: (n) Unconditional, eternal, unreasoned love. Rather than an emotion, munay is seen as an attitude of respect and appreciation for everyone and everything.

Pachamama: (n) Mother Earth, Gaia; both the physical planet and the goddess archetype. Universal feminine energy in time and space; Cosmic Mother.

Paq'o: (n) Healer, shaman in the Andean tradition who treats soul illness.

Putukusi: (n) The name of the feminine mountain just at the entrance to the ruins of Machu Picchu. Her name means *Flowering Joy.*

Yachay: (n) wisdom, the impersonal application of knowledge. Head, intuition.

Yanchay (also Llank'ay): (n) Work, labor, industriousness. It is power of action and labor.

Alison at Putukusi, the Mountain of Joy

CPSIA information can be obtained
at www.ICGtesting.com
Printed in the USA
BVHW021103141118
533114BV00001B/6/P